Word Bird's

Circus Surprise

Published in the United States of America by The Child's World®, Inc.
PO Box 326
Chanhassen, MN 55317-0326
800-599-READ
www.childsworld.com

Project Manager Mary Berendes
Editor Katherine Stevenson, Ph.D.
Designer Ian Butterworth

Library of Congress Cataloging-in-Publication Data
Moncure, Jane Belk.
Word Bird's circus surprise / by Jane Belk Moncure.
p. cm.
Summary: Simple text describes what Word Bird sees at the circus.
ISBN 1-56766-996-4 (lib. : alk. paper)
[1. Circus—Fiction. 2. Birds—Fiction.]   I. Title.
PZ7.M739 Wo 2002
[E]—dc21
2001006042

Word  Bird's™

Circus Surprise

by Jane Belk Moncure

illustrated by Chris McEwan

One day, Mama Bird
gave Word Bird a box
of polka dots…

paper,

paste,

and a pair of scissors.

"Make something pretty,"
Mama said.

Word Bird made a polka dot tie for Papa Bird…

and a polka dot hat for
Mama Bird.

Word Bird made a polka
dot clown suit to wear.

"Let's go to the circus!"
Word Bird said.
So they did.

"Hi, circus."

"Balloons. Balloons."

"Popcorn. Candy."

"Jump, lions! Jump."

"Hi, ponies."

"Prance, ponies! Prance."

"Hi, elephants."

"Hi, bear."

"Ride, bear! Ride."

"Hi, acrobats."

"Swing, acrobats!
Swing high."

"Oh no!"

"More balloons, please."

"Here come the clowns."

Clowns, clowns, funny
clowns. But where is
Word Bird?

"Surprise!"

"Laugh, clowns! Laugh."

"Bye-bye, circus."

Can you read these words with Word Bird?

polka dots

elephant

dance

paste

paper

scissors

bear

tie

acrobat

hat

clown

lion

balloon

bye-bye